ONLY
ONLY
MARISOL
RAINEY

ERIN ENTRADA KELLY

ONLY ONLY MARISOL RAINEY

GREENWILLOW BOOKS
An Imprint of HarperCollinsPublishers

Only Only Marisol Rainey
Copyright © 2023 by Erin Entrada Kelly

The text of this book is set in Garth Graphic.
Book design by Sylvie Le Floc'h

Library of Congress Cataloging-in-Publication Data

Names: Kelly, Erin Entrada, author.
Title: Only only Marisol Rainey / Erin Entrada Kelly.
Description: First edition. | New York, NY : Greenwillow Books, an imprint of HarperCollinsPublishers, 2023. | Audience: Ages 8-12. | Audience: Grades 4-6. | Summary: Marisol and her best friend Jada love to ride their bikes, except when they have to ride past a dangerous beast they call Daggers, but when Daggers gets loose, Marisol unexpectedly rescues him, conquering one of her biggest fears.
Identifiers: LCCN 2022058488 | ISBN 9780062970480 (hardback) | ISBN 9780062970503 (ebook)
Subjects: CYAC: Bicycles and bicycling—Fiction. | Best friends—Fiction. | Friendship—Fiction. | Courage—Fiction. | German shepherd dog—Fiction. | Dogs—Fiction. | Filipino Americans—Fiction.
Classification: LCC PZ7.1.K45 On 2023 | DDC [Fic]—dc23
LC record available at https://lccn.loc.gov/2022058488
23 24 25 26 27 LBC 5 4 3 2 1
First Edition

Greenwillow Books

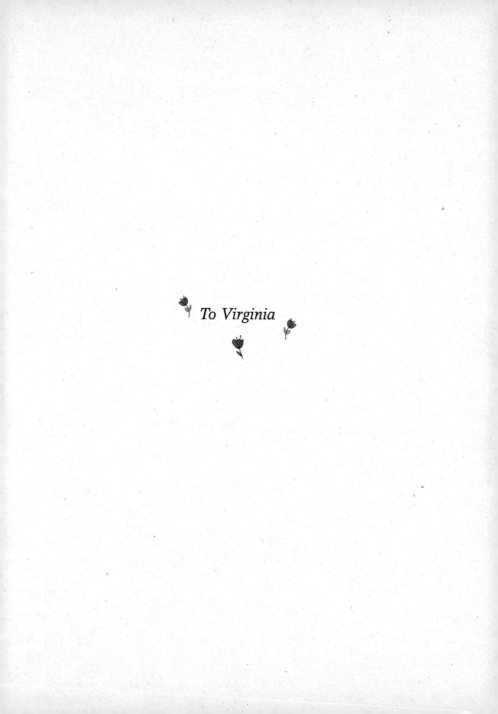

To Virginia

CONTENTS

GINNY

Marisol Rainey can do many things, but she's not good at all of them.

She can jump, but not very high.

She can run, but not very fast.

She can throw, but not very far.

Not very far

Marisol is a good Hula-Hooper, an okay mathematician, and a so-so speller.

But if there is one area in which Marisol Rainey excels, it's bike riding. If riding bikes were a subject at Getty Elementary, Marisol would get an A+. She rounds corners like a professional. Her balance is superb, like an Olympian. She can speed up, slow down, and brake at a moment's notice. She loves the way the Louisiana breeze feels on her face as she glides down the streets. When she is on her bicycle, she doesn't have a care in the world. She can ride from one end of the earth to the other. She can ride all the way to the Philippines and meet some long-lost relatives if she wanted. That's how it feels, anyway.

PHILIPPINES

Marisol believes that all important things should have names, so she has named her bike Ginny. Ginny belongs to Marisol, and only Marisol. Nothing can come between them.

Well.

Almost nothing.

THAT ONE TERRIBLE THING

Marisol loves her neighborhood. Her best friend, Jada George (whose bicycle is named Bunny), lives nearby and can come over almost any time. Her other friend, Felix, isn't far, either. Most of the streets are named for flowers or trees, which Marisol appreciates—though she would rather live in a neighborhood where the streets are named after cats.

Marisol and Jada have a favorite route for bike riding. Down Oak, right on Lily, then right on Rose. Their favorite time to explore the neighborhood is on Saturdays and Sundays. Jada goes to her dad's every other weekend, but other than that, Marisol and Jada have standing plans to ride bikes together, starting on Saturday morning.

Off they go—breeze blowing, tires rolling pleasantly across the cement, the hot sun on their skin. The oak trees tower above them and make shadows on the sidewalk. They pass Miss Penelope's flower garden, and Miss Penelope herself, if she happens to be outside. All is well . . . until they see the white fence about halfway down Rose.

That's when their eyes widen. That's when they tap their brakes.

Behind that fence is the One Terrible Thing about their neighborhood.

The thing they fear above all else.

Sometimes they pedal really, really fast, until the fence is behind them. Most times, though, they slow down and pedal really quietly and try not to look at what's on the other side of the fence.

It's not good to make eye contact—Marisol's older brother, Oz, told them that. But it's hard. They need to look because they want to be prepared in case something happens. Because they know what lurks behind the fence. It's a deadly, terrifying, bloodthirsty beast.

No, not the squirrel. That's just Reginald.

The deadly, terrifying, bloodthirsty beast is named Daggers.

Daggers has sharp teeth.

Daggers has angry eyebrows.

Daggers is very big, with pointy ears.

Daggers never moves when they ride by. He just stares and stares—and drools—like he's wondering how he can get them into his food dish.

In short: Daggers is d-a-n-g-e-r-o-u-s.

Thankfully, Daggers is also behind a fence, which prevents him from getting loose.

It would be awful, dreadful, and downright horrible if he ever broke free.

Who knows what would happen then?

WOULD YOU RATHER

In all honesty, Marisol doesn't know if Daggers is dangerous. She also doesn't know if his name is Daggers. That's just what she calls him, because the name seems fitting for a big German shepherd who likes to eat children.

"Thank goodness Daggers can't get out," says Jada as they continue down Rose Street on a particularly bright Saturday morning during spring break.

"Agreed," says Marisol.

The corner of Rose and Daisy is up ahead. It's one of Marisol's favorite corners to turn because the road is nice and smooth there. On Tulip, there's a big crack you have to avoid, and on Orchid Street, some of the cement is rocky. But the corner of Rose and Daisy is marvelous.

"Would you rather be trapped in the yard with Daggers for thirty seconds or stand next to Mr. Zhang's beehive that's been knocked over for thirty seconds?" asks Jada, over her shoulder. Jada is a philosopher, so she loves asking questions. Would You Rather is one of her favorite games.

Mr. Zhang is Marisol's neighbor. He keeps bees in his backyard. Marisol was scared of the bees for a long time after her family moved in, but Mr. Zhang told them that honeybees weren't aggressive. One day he brought a jar of honey to the Raineys

and invited Marisol and Oz to see the beehive. Oz wasn't nervous at all, but Marisol was.

"They just want to find food and get home safely," Mr. Zhang explained. "Stinging is a last resort." He told Marisol that she should stand very still if a bee came near her. "Once it realizes you're not a flower, it will go away peacefully all by itself," he said.

And it was true. It worked!

Sometimes, things are less scary when you understand them.

Even though Marisol knew a lot about the bees now, she still wouldn't want to stand next to a hive after it had been knocked over. No way. What if the bees were angry and confused and blamed the

first person they saw? Thirty seconds doesn't seem like a long time, but "time is relative," according to Marisol's mother, who is the smartest person Marisol knows.

Thirty minutes at Recess goes By REALLY fast, but thirty minutes waiting in Line moves REALLY SLOWLY...

That's Because time is Relative!

Marisol glides around the corner onto Daisy Street and decides to count to thirty before she commits to an answer. She wants to see how long it is.

One-Mississippi. Two-Mississippi. Three-Mississippi.

She hasn't even reached five-Mississippi before Jada says, "Did you hear me, Marisol?"

"Yes," Marisol replies. "I was trying to decide my answer." Bees versus Daggers is a hard decision.

"You were taking forever!" Jada says.

"Only five seconds."

Time is relative.

Marisol eventually decides she would rather stand by Mr. Zhang's toppled beehive than be trapped in a yard with Daggers.

She can't imagine *ever* being face-to-face with Daggers.

THE MOST DISTURBING
FLYER IN THE WORLD

By the following week, Marisol has already forgotten about playing Would You Rather with Jada and choosing bees over Daggers. But then Marisol, Mrs. Rainey, and Marisol's big brother, Oz, walk out of the house to run errands and Marisol immediately notices something tucked under Charlie's windshield.

Charlie is the name of Mrs. Rainey's sedan.

No one else knows this. Only Marisol.

CHARLIE CHAPLIN,
Silent film star

CHARLIE CHAPLIN,
Mrs. Rainey's sedan

Oz spots the flyer, too. He reaches over and snatches it up.

"What is it?" Mrs. Rainey asks as she gets into the car.

"Someone lost their dog," says Oz. He and Marisol climb into the backseat. Oz thinks he's old enough to sit in the front, but Mrs. Rainey says he can't for another year at least.

"Let me see," Marisol says. Oz doesn't give her the paper right away because sometimes he likes to be super annoying for no reason whatsoever. Marisol is forced to take initiative, so she grabs it out of his hands, takes one look at the paper, and everything comes to a screeching halt.

Not really. But it feels like it.

Marisol's whole world suddenly stops. Her heart. Her breathing. Her ability to move. The neighborhood going by outside the car window. But only Marisol notices.

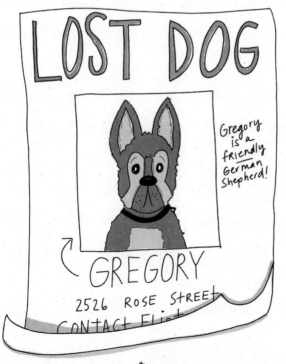

Daggers is on the loose.

Only his name isn't Daggers. It turns out it's Gregory.

"Who names their dog Gregory, anyway?" Oz says. "If I had a German shepherd, I'd name it Bloodborn. 'Gregory' doesn't sound scary at all."

Bloodborn is one of the characters from *Knights of Redemption,* Oz's favorite video game.

Marisol doesn't say a word. Instead, she looks out the window. There are so many places for a dog to hide. Behind the bushes. Behind the trees. Behind the houses. And she doesn't care if the dog's real name is Gregory or that the flyer describes him as friendly. *Maybe he's friendly at home,* Marisol thinks. *But that doesn't mean he's friendly with everyone.*

Surely no one can be friendly all the time. Not even a dog.

Besides, Marisol has never once seen Daggers— er, Gregory—wag his tail. Isn't that what dogs do when they are happy?

Her heart thumps.

Tha-thump. Tha-thump. Tha-thump.

Gregory could be anywhere.

Anywhere.

BUT FIRST

Marisol's friend Felix Powell claims he can talk to animals. Jada doesn't believe him, but Marisol does.

At least she *thinks* she does.

"Everyone knows people can't talk to animals," says Jada as they ride their bikes to the Powells' the next Saturday. The missing-dog flyer is folded up in Marisol's back pocket. "So I don't know why we're asking Felix for help."

Marisol has trouble concentrating on what

Jada is saying, because she's too busy looking to the left, to the right, and over her shoulder. She doesn't feel free and happy, like she usually does when she rides her bike. In fact, she hasn't ridden Ginny ever since she found the flyer. But she and Jada made a promise to look out for each other, and that's exactly what they're doing now. It makes Marisol feel a little bit better, but part of her still feels she has a big, enormous bull's-eye on her back.

The Powells live in a small one-story house on the corner of Rose and Amaryllis. When Marisol and Jada pull up, they lay Ginny and Bunny on the grass, then walk cautiously to the front door. They've never been on Felix's porch before. Going to someone's house for the first time is always a new adventure.

Marisol clears her throat so she can sound as polite as possible. Felix lives with his grandmother—whom he calls Nan—and Marisol wants to make a good impression.

Nan opens the door. She's wearing a long floral dress. Marisol thinks it's pretty, but she's too shy to say so.

"Hi, Ms. . . ." Marisol pauses. She doesn't know what to call Felix's grandmother. Should she call her "Nan" too? Or something else? "Ms. . . . uh . . . Ms. Nan. Is Felix home? We were wondering if he wanted to ride bikes with us."

Nan smiles. "Yes, he's home. But I don't think he'll be able to ride bikes."

Marisol wants to ask why, but she doesn't want to sound nosy.

Nan turns around and calls out, "Felix! Your friends are here!"

Felix's dog, Mary Puppins, runs around the corner of the living room at the sound of visitors and bounds onto the porch with Felix behind her.

"Careful, Puppins!" he says as Jada squeals with delight. Mary Puppins is cute and small and sounds like a squeak toy when she barks. Marisol has never heard Gregory bark, but she's certain it wouldn't sound like a squeak toy.

Mary Puppins's tail is wagging so hard that her bottom shakes. Jada bends down so she can scratch the little dog behind the ears before Nan shoos Mary Puppins back in the house.

Mary Puppins

Nan goes inside, too.

"Don't want to waste the air conditioning!" Nan says before she closes the door.

Mrs. Rainey says the same thing when Marisol or Oz leave the door open too long.

Felix is smiling from ear to ear, even though he has no idea why Marisol and Jada are there. Felix is one of the smiliest people Marisol knows.

"Hi!" Felix says. "What's up?"

"Do you want to ride bikes with us?" asks Marisol.

This is the first time Marisol and Jada have invited Felix to ride bikes, so he looks confused for a moment. Then he says, "I would, but I can't."

"Why?" Jada asks. "Are you busy or something?"

"No," Felix says. "I mean, I *can't*. I don't know how."

Marisol raises her eyebrows. She thought everyone knew how to ride bikes. Jada is surprised, too. She even gasps.

"Ay naku," Marisol mutters. *Ay naku* is a Filipino expression that means something like "oh my goodness." Mrs. Rainey says it all the time, usually under her breath.

"You don't know how to ride a bike?" Jada says. "No one ever taught you?"

Felix shrugs, like it's no big deal. Nothing is ever a big deal to Felix. Marisol wishes she was more like that. Sometimes she feels like everything is a big deal.

"My nan doesn't know how to ride a bike, and

I live with my nan," Felix says. "There's no one to teach me."

Marisol remembers when she learned to ride a bike. Her dad taught her. He is only home one week out of every month because he works offshore in the Gulf of Mexico as an electrician on an oil rig. He spent three of his at-home days teaching her.

Marisol and Jada say, "We'll teach you," in unison.

That's the thing about best friends. Sometimes you say the exact same thing at the exact same time.

Felix's face lights up. "Really?"

"Yes," Marisol says. "Really." She clears her throat. "But first, we need you to do something." She pauses. "We need you to talk to an animal for us."

FRANKLY

Felix claims he has conversations with Mary Puppins all the time. That's why Marisol wanted to go to Felix's house in the first place. Surely he can talk to big, scary dogs just as easily as small, friendly ones.

Only it turns out that the animal must be in front of you. That's what Felix says. Or nearby, at least. And no one knows where Daggers is.

"There's nothing I can do," Felix says. He shakes his head woefully. "If Gregory isn't

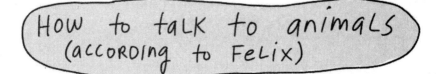

How to talk to animals
(according to Felix)

Study them CLOSELY.

Imagine what it's like to be them.

BLOCK everything out and CONCENTRATE.

What's your favorite type of music?

Hip-Hop!

Start a conversation.

here, I'm not able to talk to him."

Jada crosses her arms. "Frankly, I think the whole thing is suspect in the first place," she says.

Marisol isn't sure what *frankly* means exactly, but it sounds very grown-up at the beginning of a sentence. Jada is the third-smartest person Marisol knows, after her mom and Mrs. Ruby.

"I'm not making it up, if that's what you're getting at," Felix says.

Jada sighs. "Everyone knows people can't talk to animals, and they can't talk to us."

"That's not true," says Felix. "There was once a chimpanzee named Washoe who learned how to say hundreds of words in American Sign Language. And that's just one example."

WAYS
ANIMALS
COMMUNICATE

Cats communicate with humans by meowing. Adult cats don't meow at other cats.

MEOW.

Guinea pigs jump when they're happy. Humans call it "popcorning."

Rattlesnakes rattle their tails to say "GO AWAY!"

ch-ch-ch
ch-ch-ch

"You know what I mean," Jada says.

Marisol shifts from foot to foot nervously and glances at the street behind her. They are still on the porch. Daggers could be anywhere.

"Maybe—*maybe*—if you concentrate *really*

hard, Daggers—uh, Gregory—will communicate with you," Marisol says. "You know, through the universe or something."

Felix shrugs. "Maybe. But I've never done that before, so I'm not sure." He glances between Marisol and Jada. "Will you still teach me how to ride a bike, even if it doesn't work?"

This time, Marisol and Jada have different answers.

Felix smiles, because he's decided that he likes Marisol's answer better.

WHAT NOW?

With Daggers—aka Gregory—on the loose, Marisol only feels safe at home. So Marisol, Jada, and Felix walk together back to the Raineys' house. It's much more fun to ride a bike than to walk one, but Felix says he doesn't want to ride on the back of one of their bikes because it makes him too nervous. Instead, he offers to push Ginny so Marisol doesn't have to. Marisol thinks this is a nice gesture.

It takes a *relatively* long time to get to the Raineys'. Marisol spends most of the walk scanning the neighborhood just in case Gregory is hiding behind one of the bushes. Her heart *tha-thumps, tha-thumps* the whole way.

When they finally arrive, they make a beeline to the kitchen for tall glasses of cold water. They are hot, especially after all that walking. Mrs. Rainey smiles at them and says hello to Felix. She's sitting at the kitchen table, working on her laptop.

"We're going to teach Felix how to ride a bike," Marisol announces.

"In exchange for my animal whispering services," adds Felix.

Mrs. Rainey raises her eyebrows.

"I don't have a bike of my own," Felix says. "So they're letting me use theirs."

"Wonderful," Mrs. Rainey says. She taps the side of her head. "Once you know how to ride a bike, you never forget. It's locked in your brain forever."

Jada finishes her water. "You're not using *my* bike," she says, shaking her head. "No one gets on Bunny but me."

Marisol looks at Felix. "We'll use Ginny."

A few minutes later, they're all standing in the driveway around Ginny. Marisol pats Ginny's red banana seat the same way her dad did when he taught her how to ride.

"Hop on," she says to Felix.

Jada stands next to Bunny with her arms crossed.

Felix takes the handlebars and wobbles his way up onto the seat. He has a crease between his eyebrows, which makes him look a little worried and makes Marisol feel better. Sometimes she feels like the only one in the whole world who worries.

"You're not going to just push me into the street or anything, are you?" Felix asks.

"Of course not," Marisol says.

"When my mom taught me how to ride, she didn't give me any warning. She just"—Jada raises her hands in the air, like she's releasing invisible handlebars—"let go."

Felix's eyes are as round as saucers. "You won't do that, will you, Marisol?"

"Of course not," repeats Marisol. She gives Jada a look that says *don't scare Felix.* Jada shrugs with one shoulder.

"What next, then?" Felix asks.

Marisol purses her lips. *"Hmm."*

"Yeah," Jada says. "Was jetzt?" Which means "What now?" in German. Marisol and Jada don't speak German—not really—but one weekend they spent hours memorizing words and phrases in different languages so they could speak in code. *Was jetzt?* was one of the phrases they learned.

Marisol frowns because she doesn't know the answer to *Was jetzt?*

She's never taught anyone how to ride a bike before.

"Let's take a break," she says. She is proud of herself for speaking with authority, even though they're not really taking a break from anything since they just got started. "Let's try to communicate with Gregory from the backyard for a while, and we'll come back to Ginny later."

The backyard is safer, she thinks to herself.

But no one can hear Marisol's thoughts.

Only Marisol.

FOR THE RECORD

Felix, Marisol, and Jada are sitting cross-legged in Marisol's backyard. The birds are chirping. The sun is shining. All three of them have sweat beads on their foreheads. Marisol and Jada are looking at Felix, and Felix is looking at the ground because it helps him concentrate better.

"For the record," Felix says, without looking up, "I don't think this is going to work. How can you have a conversation with someone when they're not sitting next to you?"

"People have conversations from far away all the time," says Jada. "Telephones, email, text messages—"

"I don't think Gregory has a phone," Felix says.

"It doesn't matter, anyway," Jada says. "Because you can't really talk to animals in the first place."

Felix's head snaps up. "I can, too. Just because you don't believe something doesn't mean it isn't true."

Jada rolls her eyes. "It doesn't make *logical sense*, Felix. Humans and animals don't have conversations."

"Jane Goodall had conversations with

chimpanzees," Felix says matter-of-factly. "And besides, humans *are* animals."

Jane Goodall is a famous primatologist. She was the first scientist to give names to the chimpanzees, like Flint, Frodo, Flo and Goliath.

Marisol claps her hands, just like Mrs. Ruby does when she wants everyone to "simmer down." "Frankly," Marisol says, "I think we should try to figure out where Daggers—I mean, *Gregory*—is, even if it doesn't work."

Jada crosses her arms.

Felix closes his eyes and calls out, "Gregory! Here, Gregory!"

The big enormous bull's-eye on Marisol's back burns. What if Gregory comes charging down Oak Street, leaps over the fence, and eats all of them for lunch?

Actually, it's too late for lunch. It'd be more like an early dinner.

Marisol swallows. She has a huge, nervous lump right in the middle of her throat.

She waits and waits and waits.

Tha-thump, tha-thump, tha-thump.

"This is stupid," Jada says.

Marisol thinks Jada might be hurting Felix's feelings, but Felix only shrugs.

"I told you it probably wouldn't work," he says. "Like I said, Gregory has to be right in front of me."

Marisol is disappointed. All this hard work for nothing. *There must be something worthwhile we can do with Felix here*, Marisol thinks.

Marisol's face lights up. "I know, let's go talk to Beans!"

Felix jumps to his feet. He's excited.

Not Jada, though.

She takes her time going back into the Raineys' house.

GOODY, GOODY, GUMDROPS

Felix, Marisol, and Jada are sitting cross-legged on the floor in Marisol's room. Beans, Marisol's orange cat, is in the center of their circle. Beans is very happy, because all three of them are petting him. His purrs are so loud, they fill the whole room.

"What is Beans thinking?" Marisol asks Felix.

Beans meows.

"He's thinking, 'I love attention!'" Jada says.

"No, he's not," says Felix. "He's thinking, 'I would love a ball of yarn.'"

Jada rolls her eyes. "No he *isn't*. Beans doesn't even play with yarn."

"I know," Felix says, scratching Beans on the back. "That's why he wants some. He's never played with it before, and he's heard that's what cats do."

"I don't think we have any yarn," Marisol says.

"He also says he's hungry," Felix adds.

"Big deal," Jada says. "Beans is always hungry."

Beans meows and yawns.

Felix looks around Marisol's room, but he never stops petting Beans. He's multitasking.

"You have a lot of stuffed animals," Felix says.

"Their names are Banana Split, Nacho, Lumpia, Hi-C, and Pot Roast," Marisol says, proudly. "I named them after my favorite foods. I got most of them from the claw machine at Dazzo's."

Felix's face brightens. "I love the claw machine!"

"I have a stuffed dog named Cornelius," Jada says. She pushes away from the circle and leans back against the wall. "Marisol won him for me in the claw machine, and she gave him to me because we're *very best friends.*"

Jada and Cornelius

"Nice," says Felix. "I don't have any stuffed animals. I have a lot of books, though. Nan goes to the thrift store once a week and she always brings books home."

"Goody, goody, gumdrops," Jada says dryly.

Marisol thinks Jada is being very rude to Felix, and she doesn't understand why. Jada isn't rude, usually.

"Nan is probably waiting for me to get home, so I better go," Felix says. He stands up and looks at Jada, then Marisol. "You'll give me another bike-riding lesson, right?"

Marisol isn't sure she's a good teacher, but she nods anyway.

Jada doesn't say a word, so Marisol says, "Right!" and smiles as wide as she can.

SOMETIMES WE FALL

Marisol may not know Daggers's whereabouts at this very moment, but she knows exactly where her dad is. He calls three nights a week at 7:00 p.m. on the dot, and tonight is one of those nights. Mrs. Rainey's laptop chimes from the dining-room table and then Dad's head appears on the screen. Marisol and Oz call him "Dadhead." He is sitting in the mess hall (which is what the workers on the oil rig call the cafeteria), wearing his coveralls.

DaD HeaD

Usually, Oz starts talking right away—about soccer; his best friend, Stu; or even his video game, *Knights of Redemption*—but tonight Marisol is determined to get Dadhead's attention first. She wants to tell him about Daggers.

"Guess what, Dad!" she says, elbowing Oz out of the way so she can be the main focus on Dadhead's screen. Mrs. Rainey is nearby at the kitchen sink, washing out her coffee mug, so Oz is the only one Marisol has to compete with for Dadhead's attention. "Daggers got loose and no one knows where he is!"

Dadhead's eyebrows furrow. "What is Daggers?"

Oz sighs and leans forward, blocking Marisol's face. "It's the German shepherd who lives a few blocks down. And his name *isn't* Daggers. It's Gregory."

"Oh," Dadhead says. "That's too bad. I hope they find him."

That wasn't the response Marisol was expecting. She expected her dad to say something like *Oh no! A vicious dog is on the loose! Close all the windows and lock all the doors!* or *Never leave the house until this monster is apprehended!* Was she the only one who was afraid?

Mrs. Rainey walks over to the table before Marisol can say anything else about Daggers. She tilts her head into the frame, still drying her coffee mug.

"Marisol is teaching her friend Felix how to ride a bike," she announces. She smiles broadly, like this is a great accomplishment, then goes back to the sink.

Only it's not an accomplishment at all, since Marisol doesn't know the first thing about teaching someone how to ride a bicycle.

"I don't know the first thing about teaching someone how to ride a bicycle," admits Marisol. She quickly adds, "But I'm trying my best."

"The first step is to make sure Felix is all geared

up," Dadhead says. "That means he's wearing his helmet and his elbow and kneepads. His parents will be upset if he comes home injured."

helmEt

ELBoW pads

BiCYCLE GEAR

gloves

KneepADS

"Felix doesn't live with his parents," Marisol says. "He lives with his nan."

"Well, I'm sure his nan doesn't want him to be injured, either," Dadhead says.

Marisol nods thoughtfully. She forgot to make sure Felix was geared up earlier today. Maybe it was a good thing that they didn't get very far in the riding lesson, after all.

"Felix probably doesn't have any elbow pads or kneepads, and I bet he doesn't have a helmet, either," Marisol says, frowning.

"He can borrow my old ones," Oz says. He's scrolling through his phone, waiting for his turn to tell Dadhead about his day.

Marisol almost scrunches up her nose, thinking about Oz's old sweaty elbow and kneepads and stinky helmet, but she doesn't want to seem ungrateful, so she says thank you.

"What's the next step?" Marisol asks.

"Next, you want to make sure the seat is adjusted for his height," Dadhead says. "Then, let Felix get comfortable. He might want to pedal with one foot and keep the other one on the ground, just so he can see what it feels like. He can scoot around for a bit. Eventually, when Felix is ready, he can pedal slowly while you hold the handlebars. He'll be wobbly at first."

"Okay," Marisol says. "Then what?"

"You take your hands off, bit by bit, until he can balance on his own. But stay close by, just in case. He might be scared at first."

This sounds like a big job.

Maybe too big for Marisol.

What if he hurts himself, and it's all her fault?

"Make sure you're patient," Dadhead says. "You have to be very patient when you teach someone how to do something."

"Mrs. Ruby says I'm very patient," Marisol says.

Mrs. Ruby gives the best compliments. That's one of the reasons Mrs. Ruby is Marisol's number-one favorite teacher.

But Marisol knows that being patient won't prevent Felix from falling.

"What if he falls?" Marisol asks.

"That's why he needs to be geared up, so he doesn't get hurt," Dadhead says. "He might fall, but we all fall sometimes, don't we? Oz did. You did. I did. But we get back up and try again. And next thing you know, zip!" He shoots his hands toward the screen. "You're riding a bike! And once you learn, you never forget."

Marisol wishes other things were like that. If she could learn spelling and math and never forget how to do them, she'd get straight As all the time, just like Jada.

Marisol wants to keep talking to Dadhead, but she doesn't know what else to ask about teaching someone how to ride a bike, so she says, "Felix talked to Beans today. He said Beans wants a ball of yarn."

"Oh, geez," Oz groans. "Get serious."

Marisol ignores him and looks at her mother. "Do we have any yarn, Mom?"

"Not that I know of," Mrs. Rainey says. Her coffee cup is all clean and dry. Now she's measuring her coffee grounds for tomorrow.

Mrs. Rainey takes her coffee very seriously.

Marisol turns back to Dadhead. "Once I get a ball of yarn, we'll see if Felix was right."

"Sounds like a great plan, Scraps," Dadhead says.

Marisol smiles. Scraps is her dad's pet name for Marisol. It's from one of Marisol's favorite old movies called *A Dog's Life*. Mr. Rainey doesn't call anyone else Scraps.

Only Marisol.

BEING CAUTIOUS ISN'T
A BAD THING

Later that night, Marisol is in bed with Beans and her stuffed animals. Her nightlight casts a nice glow in her room. If she had it her way, she'd leave all the lights on, but Mrs. Rainey says that's not practical.

It's not that late, but it's late enough. Beans is curled on the bed, licking his paws. Marisol's brain is full of thoughts.

Marisol's Thoughts

She mostly thinks about Daggers—er, Gregory. She wonders where he is. She wonders if he'll be waiting for her in the morning with all his teeth. She wonders, too, how he got out in the first place.

Did he see a delicious second grader that he wanted for a snack?

Was he angry at being trapped behind the

(HOW DAGGERS got out)

fence, and desperate for escape?

Did he get tired of sitting and staring, and decide to cause mayhem?

Did a huge pack of vicious, sharp-toothed dogs set him free?

What was it that lured him out and set him loose in the neighborhood?

When someone knocks on Marisol's bedroom door, she's so tense, she jumps. Pot Roast and Hi-C tumble to the floor.

Mrs. Rainey pokes her head in. "Still awake?"

Technically, it's Marisol's bedtime. But she hardly ever goes to sleep right on time. There's too much to think about.

"Yep," Marisol says.

Mrs. Rainey comes in and closes the door softly behind her. Then she sits on the bed.

She casts a shadow on the wall because of the nightlight. Beans isn't too pleased about being disturbed. He jumps up and moves closer to Marisol.

"I was thinking about Gregory," Mrs. Rainey says. "He's a big dog."

Marisol's heart goes *tha-thump.*

"Are you scared of him, too?" Marisol asks.

Mrs. Rainey smiles. "No. His owners have been posting about him online, and Gregory sounds very friendly. He's old, too. They're super worried about him."

Marisol doesn't say anything.

She already knows that his owners think he's friendly.

It doesn't make her feel any better.

What if he doesn't like strangers? Maybe Gregory is friendly to his owners, but that doesn't mean he's friendly to Marisols.

"But," Mrs. Rainey adds. "I understand why you'd be afraid of him. German shepherds are big, and they can look scary. Even if someone *tells* you their dog is friendly, that doesn't mean you won't be afraid of them anymore."

Marisol stays quiet.

"And there are certainly dogs out there who *aren't* friendly, so it's good that you're cautious,"

Mrs. Rainey adds. "Being cautious isn't a bad thing."

"Is 'cautious' the same as 'scared'?" Marisol asks.

"Sometimes," Mrs. Rainey says.

"Okay," Marisol says. "In that case, I'm very *cautious* of Gregory."

Mrs. Rainey nods. "I understand." She pauses. "Would it make you feel better if I taught you how to interact with dogs that you don't know? That way, you'll have a plan, just in case you see Gregory."

Marisol thinks about this.

Yes, she decides.

It would make her feel *much* better if she had a plan.

After all, she can't control what Gregory does. But she *can* control what she—Marisol—does.

How to introduce yourself to a Dog
Pay attention to the dog's body language. Make sure the tail is relaxed. Don't approach a dog if it's growling or if its hair is standing up.
Avoid direct eye contact. Some dogs think it's a sign of aggression.

Gently Bring your Hand forward in a closed fist so the Dog can sniff you. Don't Leave your fingers exposed. They might get nibbled.
If the dog backs away, leave it alone. If it seems comfortable, gently pet under the chin or on the chest. Some Dogs get nervous when hands move directly toward their faces, so don't pet the tops of their heads.
Remember, always be aware of a Dog's Body Language!

THE LOOKOUT

The next day, Felix is going to meet Marisol and Jada at the end of Tulip Street. There's a small empty parking lot there, so they can practice bike riding without any cars nearby. It also makes Marisol feel safe because there aren't many places for Gregory to hide.

Then again, there aren't many places for *her* to hide, either.

She decides not to think about that.

Jada has a basket on her bicycle, so Marisol puts

Oz's old gear in it. It's all washed and disinfected, thanks to Mrs. Rainey. The gear is almost as good as new.

Jada had frowned when Marisol stuffed everything into Bunny's basket.

"It's boring teaching Felix how to ride a bike," she'd said. "I'd rather do something else, like make our own movies."

But Marisol doesn't think it's boring. Besides, they made a promise—even though Felix technically couldn't keep up his end of the bargain. It wasn't his fault that he couldn't communicate with Gregory.

When they reach the parking lot, Felix is already there. Marisol suggests that Jada can be a lookout. *Maybe she won't be bored if she has an important job,* Marisol thinks.

"Look out for what?" Jada asks.

"For cars," Marisol says. "And maybe for Gregory. Just in case he shows up or something."

Marisol hasn't told anyone how scared she is of Gregory. Jada knows, though, because Jada knows everything about Marisol.

Jada doesn't seem as scared. She's mostly annoyed.

"Being a lookout is boring!" she says.

"You don't have to be a lookout," Felix says as he slips on Oz's bicycle helmet. "I'm not going anywhere near the street. I'm staying in the parking lot."

"I still think someone should be a lookout," Marisol says as she adjusts the bicycle seat for Felix's height. "Just in case."

The seat makes a funny noise when Felix sits on it, which makes him and Marisol laugh. Jada sighs loudly and walks to the edge of the parking lot to start her lookout duty.

Felix practices getting on and off. He's pretty good at it. He's too nervous to pedal, though.

"Maybe I'll pedal next time," he says. "Maybe."

Marisol doesn't mind. "It takes time to learn something new," she says. Marisol knows this for a fact, because sometimes it takes her longer than other people to learn new things. "And it takes a lot of patience."

"I'm working on being more patient," Felix says. He's unbuckling Oz's helmet now because he's done for the day. It's probably for the best because it's *so hot* outside. Marisol's shirt is sticking to her back.

"Jane Goodall says that's one of the most important things about being a primatologist," Felix adds.

"What's a primatologist?" Marisol asks.

"Someone who studies primates, like gorillas and chimpanzees," Felix says. "That's what I'm

Jane Goodall, primatologist

going to be when I grow up. What about you?"

Marisol frowns as she wheels Ginny next to Bunny and sets down the kickstand. "I don't know," she admits.

She wishes she had a better answer. Felix wants to be a primatologist, which sounds very important. And Marisol knows what Jada wants to be—a philosopher. Jada wants to teach at a college, like her parents.

Right now, though, she's collecting pebbles at the edge of the parking lot.

When Marisol and Felix walk up to her, Jada's face is sweaty and frowny.

"Thank you for being the lookout," Felix says. "What should we do now?"

Jada tosses the pebbles on the ground. "Being a lookout is the most boring job ever," she says.

"I'd rather spend all day with Evie Smythe than be a lookout."

Evie Smythe is in their grade at school. She is their nemesis because she's not very nice to Marisol. Every time Marisol sees Evie Smythe, she gets nervous, because Evie likes to hurt Marisol's feelings.

Marisol couldn't imagine spending an entire day with Evie Smythe!

"You don't have to be the lookout anymore," Marisol says. "Our lesson is over."

Jada crosses her arms and looks at Felix. "So you know how to ride a bike now?"

"Not exactly," Felix says. "I need more lessons."

"Ugh!" Jada says.

Marisol looks at the pebbles scattered on the concrete. She wishes she knew why Jada is so upset. Was being a lookout really *that* bad?

Maybe it's the weather.

The Louisiana heat can make people very grumpy.

"Thank you for being a lookout," Felix says again.

Jada uncrosses her arms, but she doesn't say anything.

"Now what should we do?" Marisol asks.

"Let's go to my house and teach Mary Puppins how to roll over," Felix says.

"Great idea!" Marisol says. Being inside sounds cooler. And safer.

"I want to go to your house and make movies in the backyard," Jada says, looking directly at

Marisol. "That sounds way more fun."

Felix frowns. "I thought you liked Mary Puppins."

Marisol doesn't know what to do. She doesn't want Jada to be upset, but she isn't in the mood to make movies. She wants to be inside, with the air conditioning, where she knows Gregory won't eat them.

She chooses a compromise.

"Let's go to Felix's first and then decide what we want to do next," says Marisol. "Maybe we can make movies later."

Jada doesn't say anything, but Marisol can tell she's not happy with the compromise.

That's the thing about best friends. Sometimes you know how the other person feels, even if they don't say it out loud.

AT FELIX'S HOUSE

Felix's house is nothing like Marisol's or Jada's. It's smaller, for one thing. But it's very nice and comfortable. There are pictures of Felix all over the walls. Here is Felix as a baby, smiling. Here is Felix as a toddler, smiling. Here is Felix in a Halloween costume, smiling. There are pictures of Felix and Nan, Felix and people Marisol doesn't know, Felix going down slides, and Felix holding Mary Puppins.

Marisol likes Felix's house right away. And she likes Nan, too.

"Hello, all!" Nan says when they come in. She has a big smile on her face, like she's thrilled to see them. She's in the living room, standing behind a recliner, flipping through a stack of mail. "How are the lessons going?"

"Slowly," Jada replies.

"But we're getting there," Marisol adds.

There are lots of pillows and blankets on the couch, like it's ready for anyone to be comfortable at any moment. Felix tells them they can sit wherever they want. Marisol sits on the couch. Jada sits on the floor. Felix doesn't sit anywhere, because Mary Puppins comes charging into the room and makes a beeline straight for him.

Felix drops to his knees so she can jump up and kiss his face.

"That dog loves Felix," Nan says. The envelopes go *flip, flip, flip*. Nan is smiley, like Felix, but every now and then she gets a line between her eyebrows as she looks at the mail.

Jada leans forward so she can pet Mary Puppins. "She's so cute!" Jada says. Marisol is happy to see Jada smiling, since she was so grumpy earlier.

Marisol wants to pet Mary Puppins too, but she's being cautious. She's not afraid, but she's also not sure what to expect. Mary Puppins seems excitable and hyperactive. What if she bites Marisol by accident or jumps up and scratches her? Marisol thinks about using all the new techniques her mom taught her, but for now, she decides to sit and observe.

"We're going to teach Mary Puppins how to roll over," Felix says to Nan. But Nan doesn't hear him at first because she's looking at the mail. He repeats himself. "Did you hear, Nan? We're going to teach her how to roll over."

Nan looks up. "That sounds fun," she says. "How're you going to do that?"

None of them have an answer for that.

"Puppins doesn't know how to follow a single command, so I'm not sure how you'll get her to roll over," Nan says, smiling. "But anything's possible."

Marisol isn't sure if that's true, but she likes the sound of it.

Anything's possible.

COMPANIONABLE

The next morning, Marisol asks her mother if Gregory has been found. Mrs. Rainey follows all the neighborhood news on social media.

"Not yet," she says. "But I certainly hope they find him. His owners are very sad. They have no idea how he managed to get out."

"He probably got lonely and hungry," Marisol says. *Lonely for neighborhood children because he's hungry for a snack,* she adds silently to herself.

"I doubt that," Mrs. Rainey says. "His owners take good care of him."

It's before nine o'clock. Oz is still asleep. Mrs. Rainey wakes up before everyone. She spends the early morning at the dining room table, enjoying her coffee and breakfast. Sometimes she reads her mystery novels. Sometimes she reads things on her phone. Right now, she's reading on her phone.

Marisol scoops cat food into Beans's bowl, then she makes cereal for herself. It's cornflakes, which isn't very exciting, but she adds lots of sugar. She adds so much sugar that it looks like a little snowy mountain. Marisol stirs it in before her mother sees it.

"Me and Jada and Felix tried to teach Felix's dog how to roll over yesterday," Marisol says, carrying her bowl to the table.

"Did it work?"

Marisol sits down. "No. Nan said anything was possible, but it wasn't possible."

Mrs. Rainey laughs, even though Marisol hadn't meant to make a joke.

Marisol takes a big bite of cornflakes. "Can we get a ball of yarn for Beans?"

"Sure," says Mrs. Rainey. "I can get a ball of yarn next time I run errands."

Marisol wants to ask when that will be, but she knows it will make her mother sigh, so she decides not to. Instead, she thinks about Gregory again.

"Do German shepherds come from Germany?"

Marisol asks as she chews. *Crunch, crunch, crunch.*

Marisol likes to ask her mother questions because Mrs. Rainey is a science teacher, which means she's very smart, and Marisol is very curious. This is another one of her special gifts, according to Mrs. Ruby. One day, Marisol asked Mrs. Ruby three questions in a row about the solar system and Mrs. Ruby said, "You're very curious, Marisol. What a special gift."

Marisol likes being curious, even if it makes her brain feel busy sometimes.

Mrs. Rainey looks up the answer on her phone. She's smart, but she doesn't know *everything.* Who does?

"It says here that German shepherds were first bred in Germany," Mrs. Rainey says. "They

Marisol's Curious Brain

are herding dogs, so that's why they're called shepherds."

Marisol raises her eyebrows. *"Hurting* dogs?" she asks with her spoon halfway between the bowl and her mouth.

"No, herding. H-E-R-D-I-N-G," Mrs. Rainey explains. "It means they gather other animals together, like sheep or cattle."

"But there aren't any sheep or cattle here."

"German shepherds also make good pets," Mrs. Rainey says. She looks at her phone and reads: "German shepherds are known for being loyal, courageous, and confident."

Loyal, courageous, confident.

"I didn't know specific dogs were known for specific things," Marisol says. It's like they have their own special gifts.

COMMON Dog TRAits

"Oh, sure. Certain dogs are known for certain things," Mrs. Rainey says. "Name another type of dog, and we'll find out what that one is known for."

Marisol takes a bite of cornflakes. She thinks and chews at the same time. Finally, she swallows and says, "Beagle."

Mrs. Rainey searches for beagle and reads: "Beagles are known for being happy, lovable, and companionable." She takes a sip of her coffee.

Too bad Gregory isn't a beagle, Marisol thinks.

"What about a weenie dog?" Marisol asks.

"Those are called dachshunds," Mrs. Rainey says. She narrows her eyes and says, "I can never remember how to spell *dachshund*."

This makes Marisol happy. Her mom is smart, and even *she* has trouble spelling words sometimes.

"Here we go," Mrs. Rainey says. She reads: "Smart, vigilant, and bold."

"What does *vigilant* mean?" Marisol asks. She pushes cornflakes out of the way and scoops at the milk in the bottom of her bowl. That's where all the sugar settles.

"When you're being vigilant, it means you're being watchful and alert. Cautious."

"Like me," Marisol says. She remembers what her mother told her. *Being cautious isn't a bad thing.*

"Yes." Mrs. Rainey smiles. "Like you."

"I'm not very bold, though. And I don't know if I'm smart." She doesn't make straight As like Jada. "So I guess I'm not a dachshund."

"You're smart," Mrs. Rainey says matter-of-factly. "And *bold* is relative."

Like time is relative, Marisol thinks. She slurps a spoonful of sugary milk.

"I'm not like a German shepherd or beagle, either," Marisol says. She shares some traits with them, but not others. She's loyal, but she doesn't think she's very confident or courageous. And

she's happy like a beagle, mostly. And lovable.
She's not sure about companionable, though.
Mostly because she's not one hundred percent
sure what *companionable* means.

"Companionable" means "pleasant, friendly, and easy to be with"

"Let's see what kind of dog you are," Mrs. Rainey says. She types something into her phone. Marisol leans over to see what, but she's too late.

"According to my estimations, you are a Cavalier King Charles spaniel," Mrs. Rainey says. She shows Marisol the phone so she can see what a Cavalier King Charles spaniel looks like. They're very cute. Not scary at all.

"Sweet, gentle, and affectionate," Mrs. Rainey explains.

Marisol smiles.

She's happy to be a Cavalier King Charles spaniel.

Cavalier King Charles Spaniel

C'EST LA VIE

Later that day, Jada and Marisol meet Felix at the parking lot again for their next lesson. As Felix gets geared up, Marisol tells Jada she doesn't have to be the lookout if she doesn't want to, even though she wishes someone would keep an eye out for Gregory.

"I'm going to ride Bunny up and down the street," says Jada, hopping on her bicycle. "I don't want to waste away the afternoon just standing around."

Marisol and Felix watch Jada pedal down the street.

"Is Jada mad at me?" Felix asks.

"Why?" Marisol says. "Did you do something?" She hopes he has an answer.

"No," Felix says. "But it seems like she's mad at me."

Marisol isn't sure what to say to this, so she doesn't say anything.

"Oh, well." Felix shrugs and gets on the bicycle. "C'est la vie."

"What does *c'est la vie* mean?"

"It means 'that's life' in French."

That's life. Marisol tucks this new phrase in her brain, so she can share it with Jada later.

Marisol wonders if "c'est la vie" is Felix's motto, since nothing seems to bother him. He didn't mind when Jada said it was "stupid" that they were trying to talk to Gregory. He didn't mind that he'd never learned how to ride a bike. He doesn't care that some of the kids at school, including Jada, don't think he can really talk to animals.

Marisol wishes she were more like Felix.

Marisol is bothered by a lot of things.

"I'll go to the end and back," Felix says.

The parking lot isn't very big, but it takes Felix a long time to go to the end and back, because he's not actually riding—he has both sneakers on the ground, and he's scooting along without sitting on the seat. It takes some maneuvering, too, because the pedals keep hitting his legs. Jada circles back toward them and takes off again before Felix returns to where Marisol is standing.

"Let's try riding it with the pedals now," Marisol suggests.

"Okay," Felix says. He gets on the banana seat but keeps one foot on the ground.

"Put both feet on the pedals," Marisol says patiently. "I'll hold Ginny."

"Okay," Felix says. He hesitates at first, then puts his other foot on the pedal. He's gripping the handlebars with all his might. Ginny is wobbly, but Marisol holds on tight. She knows how scary it can be to balance by yourself for the first time.

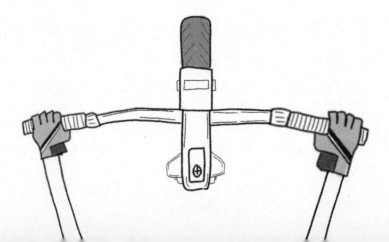

"You can pedal now," Marisol says. "I'll hold on so you don't fall off."

Felix looks at his feet and the handlebars and the parking lot in front of him. "You promise you won't let go?" he asks.

"I promise," Marisol says. She means it, too.

Felix turns the pedals slowly, slowly. He jerks the handlebars side to side, but Marisol doesn't let go.

They don't get very far, though. Felix puts his feet down.

"Sorry," he says.

No one says anything for a bit.

Sometimes, when Mrs. Rainey feels particularly overwhelmed, she says, "I need a moment," and it means that Oz and Marisol should leave her alone for a little while.

It seems like Felix needs a moment. Marisol decides to focus on a collection of acorns on the ground nearby. She wonders if a squirrel dropped them there.

After a few quiet seconds, Felix puts his feet back up and they try again.

And again.

And again.

But Felix never gets very far.

"I don't want to fall," Felix says.

Marisol understands. She felt the same way when she learned how to ride her bike.

They try again and get a little farther, but Felix is still too nervous to make any real progress. He sighs, gets off the bike, and unbuckles the helmet as Marisol puts down the kickstand.

"It's okay," Marisol says. "It takes time."

Felix puts the helmet on the ground so he can take off his other gear. His hair is all sweaty.

Jada is coming back around again. She's riding with one hand.

"Are you done finally?" Jada asks. She zips right up, puts on the brake, and stops in front of them.

Marisol is about to answer, but Felix speaks instead.

"It's stupid anyway," he says. His voice sounds different. Once he has all the gear off, he puts it inside the helmet and shoves the helmet in Marisol's direction. His face is not smiley. He looks sad.

"What's stupid?" Marisol asks.

"Teaching me how to ride a bike," he says. "I don't even have a bike, so why should I learn how to ride one?"

Marisol takes the helmet from him. She doesn't know what to say.

"Thanks for teaching me, Marisol," Felix says. He smiles, but it's not a usual Felix smile. "You're a good teacher."

He walks off in the direction of his house.

Jada and Marisol watch him go.

A TERRIFIC IDEA

That night, Marisol is in bed with all her stuffed animals. She's staring at the ceiling, thinking about Felix. She'd never seen Felix sad before. Maybe he's not always happy, after all. Maybe things *do* bother him.

She hopes he knows he's not the only one who gets sad or mad or cranky. Marisol feels all those things. Sometimes she feels them all at the same time, or one right after the other. There are times when she's alone in bed with all her cats

and she's sure she's the only person in the world
who has jumbled feelings.

Maybe she's not, though.

Surely everyone feels jumbled from time to time.

Surely.

She thinks about Felix borrowing all of Oz's gear, and how he said there was no point in learning to ride a bike since he doesn't have one.

And then she has one feeling after the other. But they aren't jumbled.

First, she's sad that Felix doesn't have a bicycle.

Then she's excited, because an idea is forming in her mind, like puzzle pieces.

Then she's happy, because it all snaps into place.

Click, click, click.

A FANTASTIC, WONDERFUL, TERRIFIC IDEA

The next morning, Marisol sails into the kitchen.

"I have a fantastic, wonderful, terrific idea!" she announces.

Mrs. Rainey is sitting at the dining room table, eating waffles. The whole kitchen smells like waffles. Yum! Marisol feeds Beans, then gets a plate so she can build a tower of waffles and cover them with a bucket of butter and syrup.

"What's your fantastic, wonderful, terrific idea?" her mother asks.

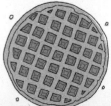

"I've been teaching Felix how to ride a bicycle, but yesterday he said he didn't want to learn anymore. He says there's no point because he doesn't have a bike to ride, anyway," Marisol says. She's talking fast because she's excited about her plan. She's also excited about the waffles. She stacks three on her plate, but her mom makes her put two of them back because she knows Marisol won't be able to eat them all.

Marisol intends to soak her waffle with as much syrup as possible, but her mother makes her stop mid-pour.

"Don't use too much," Mrs. Rainey says, without looking up. "All that sugar is bad for your teeth."

Marisol sneaks in one extra second of syrup pouring, then carries her plate to the table and sits down.

"My fantastic, wonderful, terrific idea is that we give Oz's old bike to Felix!" Marisol says. "I saw it in the garage. It's just sitting there."

Oz has a bigger bicycle now, since he's twelve.

Mrs. Rainey sips her coffee and considers this. Then she says, "That *is* a terrific idea."

"I'll ask Oz if it's okay," Marisol says. She hasn't even taken a bite of her waffle yet, but she's already up from the table and rushing to Oz's room. There's no time to waste when you have a great idea.

Marisol knocks on Oz's door and opens it before he can say anything. He's asleep. His hair sticks up in every direction. He grumbles when he hears Marisol. She fires off one word after another. She barely even notices how his room smells like dirty sneakers and sweat.

"Oz, can we give your old bike to Felix because Felix doesn't have one and you grew out of it and you don't need it anymore and you have a new bike anyway and Mom said it was a terrific idea so can we do it?"

"I don't want to give away my bike," he grumbles, without opening his eyes. He rolls over. "Go away."

"But you're not even using it!" Marisol says. "Even Mom agreed that it's a fantastic, wonderful, terrific—"

"It's *my* bike." Oz pulls the comforter to his chin.

"Mom and Dad are the ones who bought it," Marisol says, putting her hands on her hips. "Technically, it's *their* bike."

Oz puts a pillow over his head. "Go away!"

"But Felix doesn't even have a bike—"

"Ugh!"

"—and you have two bikes and one of them you're not even using—"

"I'm trying to sleep, you evil peasant!"

"—and Mom said—"

Oz grabs the pillow and tosses it in her direction, but he misses. "Fine, take the bike! *Take the bike!*"

Marisol smiles.

Triumph.

VANILLA AND SPRINKLES

Oz goes to his best friend Stu's house once he wakes up and eats a million waffles, so Marisol has Mrs. Rainey all to herself. Mrs. Rainey says they have some work to do to get the bike ready for Felix. The tires are flat, for one thing, and it needs a new chain. They load the bicycle into Charlie and take it to a bike shop. Marisol has never been in a bike shop before. It smells like rubber and there are bikes everywhere. Some of them, with shiny hardware and thick black tires, even hang from the ceiling. She hopes all the shininess in the shop doesn't hurt the old bike's feelings. It may be a silly thought, but she has it anyway. Oz's old bike doesn't even have a name.

Marisol is pushing on the brake of an expensive model when Mrs. Rainey tells her that the bike won't be ready for a couple of hours.

"Can we go to Dazzo's while we wait?" Marisol asks, before Mrs. Rainey has even finished her sentence. It's almost lunchtime, and Dazzo's is Marisol's number-one favorite restaurant. They have the best nachos in the whole world. Even better, they have a claw machine called the Comfort Zone.

Marisol is excellent at the claw machine.

Mrs. Rainey says Dazzo's is a good idea, and on the way there she even stops at a craft store to get a ball of yarn for Beans at Marisol's request.

At the restaurant, Marisol orders her food right away. She also orders a Hi-C Orange. Not all restaurants have Hi-C Orange, but Dazzo's does. Marisol hopes their food comes out quickly. She feels jumpy and impatient. She wants to play the claw machine and she wants to pick up the bike and she wants to give the bike to Felix.

No one can be patient *all the time*.

She swings her legs and looks around anxiously.

That's when she sees something awful.

Something truly terrible.

Something that makes her stomach tie itself in knots.

Her nemesis. Evie Smythe.

Marisol slides down in her chair. Evie makes fun of Marisol sometimes at school. Evie has invisible darts that she likes to throw at people. Especially Marisol.

Luckily, Evie doesn't see Marisol. She's sitting with her mom, too. Evie usually wears fox ears and brightly colored clothes. But she's not wearing her fox ears today. She's not wearing bright colors, either.

Evie

Mrs. Rainey follows Marisol's eyes and sees Evie a few tables over. Evie is Oz's friend Stu's little sister, so the entire Rainey family knows the Smythes.

"We should say hello on our way out," Mrs. Rainey says.

Marisol's eyes turn to saucers. "No way!"

Mrs. Rainey frowns. She takes a sip of water. "I know Evie isn't very nice to you, and there's no excuse for that. You don't have to talk to her if you don't want to, but I'd like to say hello. Evie's grandmother is in the hospital, and they're going through a tough time. You can play the claw machine while I chat with Mrs. Smythe."

Marisol sits up straight. She wants to ask her mom to give her five dollars, but she doesn't want to press her luck.

As it turns out, Marisol gets only two dollars. After they eat and Mrs. Rainey pays the check, Marisol goes straight to the claw machine. She doesn't even look in Evie Smythe's direction. So what if she's going through a tough time? Evie Smythe is mean. Marisol can't remember Evie ever being nice to her. Not once.

The Comfort Zone gives you four plays for one dollar, so Marisol gets eight tries. She examines the claw machine closely so she can come up with a strategy.

She decides to try for the penguin. She gets it on the third try.

On the fourth try, she gets a giraffe. And she wasn't even planning for it.

Marisol is *excellent* at the claw machine.

She snuggles her new stuffed animals close, then looks for Mrs. Rainey, who's still talking to Evie and her mom.

Oh, well, Marisol thinks. *I'll just wait here and think of good names.*

COMFORT ZONE

She examines the penguin first. It's round and cute with floppy flippers.

Marisol names all her stuffed animals after her favorite foods. She immediately knows what she'll name the penguin. Vanilla! After her favorite flavor of ice cream.

Maybe I'll name the giraffe Sprinkles, she thinks,

because that's her favorite ice cream topping.

Now that she has good names for her new stuffed animals, Marisol is anxious to leave. She wants to get Felix's bicycle. But Mrs. Rainey is still talking to the Smythes. Evie is looking at her plate. She isn't smiling. She looks like a robot that's been powered down. Mrs. Smythe is rubbing Evie's back and talking to Mrs. Rainey, but Marisol can't hear what they're saying.

Marisol wonders what's wrong with Evie's grandmother. She also wonders what it's like to have grandparents nearby. Mrs. Rainey's parents live in the Philippines. Marisol has never met them. And Mr. Rainey's parents live far away, too. It must be nice to have a grandma you can do things with.

Marisol thinks of Nan.

She studies the giraffe, then Evie.

When Marisol walks to the Smythes' table, Mrs. Rainey looks up and smiles. So does Evie's mom. Even Evie raises her head, but she doesn't smile. She doesn't frown, either.

"Hey, Marisol," Evie says. Usually, Evie's voice is sharp and mean. But not today.

Today her voice is sad and quiet.

Mrs. Rainey nods toward Marisol's prizes.

"You caught two this time!" she says.

Marisol nods. She holds Vanilla tight in the crook of her arm.

"This is Vanilla," she says. She holds the giraffe toward Evie. "I named this one Sprinkles, but you can name it whatever you want."

Evie raises her eyebrows.

"You can have it," explains Marisol. "I don't need two. I mostly just wanted the penguin, anyway. It was just luck that I got the giraffe."

Evie smiles. It's not a big, joyful, Felix-level smile, but it's genuine. Smiles can be sad, too. Just like voices.

"Thanks, Marisol," Evie says. She gently takes the giraffe from Marisol and examines him. "Sprinkles is a good name."

Mrs. Rainey winks at Marisol when no one's looking.

Marisol feels just like a Cavalier King Charles spaniel.

Evie
and
Sprinkles

MEJORES AMIGOS

Oz's old bike looks like new. After they get it home, it occurs to Mrs. Rainey that they should have checked with Nan first to make sure the plan was okay with her. Luckily, Nan agrees that it is a fantastic, wonderful, terrific idea. But she doesn't want to take the bike for free, so she offers to take family photos of the Raineys during one of Dadhead's at-home weeks. That's how Marisol finds out that Nan is a photographer, which explains all the photos at Felix's house.

Jada rides over on Bunny just as Marisol finishes taking the bike for a test run. Everything works perfectly.

"Can I come with you to bring it to Felix?" Jada asks, after Marisol tells her the plan. Nan has agreed to keep the bike a secret so Marisol can surprise him.

"Okay," Marisol says. "But don't say things like 'goody, goody, gumdrops.' Deal?"

"Deal," says Jada.

They even shake on it, right there in the driveway, with Felix's new bike between them.

"I thought you didn't like Felix," says Marisol.

Jada sighs. "It's not that I don't like him, exactly."

"It sure *seems* like you don't like him," says Marisol. "Is it because you don't believe he can talk to animals?"

"No. I don't care about that. Not really," Jada says. "I just like it better when it's only me and you. I don't want a third wheel."

"What's wrong with three wheels?" Marisol asks. "A lot of great things have three wheels."

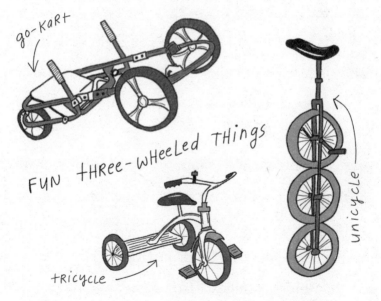

go-kart

FUN tHRee-wHeeLed THings

tRiCyCLe

unicycle

Jada lets out a big exhale. "I guess I just didn't want you to become his best friend instead of mine. I was worried you liked him more than me."

"That's impossible! How could I ever like anyone more than you?"

"I don't know." Jada shrugs. "Everyone at school likes Felix. Even Evie. And he can talk to animals. You can't beat that."

"Aha!" Marisol says. "So you *do* believe him!"

Jada zips her lips tight with her fingers, like she accidentally revealed a secret, which makes Marisol giggle.

"I would never like anyone more than you," Marisol says. "You're my number-one BFF. And that means *forever.*" She reaches her hand out for another shake. "Mejores amigos."

"Mejores amigos," Jada agrees.

That means "best friends" in Spanish.

FLINT

Marisol rides the brand-new used bike to Felix's house with Jada by her side. Marisol's insides are jittery with excitement. She makes it all the way to the Powells' before she remembers that she has a bull's-eye on her back and Gregory is still on the loose. But now she's safely on the Powells' porch, putting the kickstand down and knocking on the door, so she's not as scared as usual.

She takes a quick look around, though. Just in case.

No German shepherds in sight.

Marisol knocks on the door. Her heart races. She and Jada have big matching smiles. Surely this will be the best surprise *ever.*

When Felix opens the door, Marisol opens her arms wide and says, "Surprise!"

Jada opens her arms wide, too. "Surprise!"

Felix looks confused. His eyes move from Marisol to the bike to Jada and back to the bike again.

"What's going on?" he asks.

Marisol sees Nan behind him, walking toward the door with Mary Puppins bouncing around at her feet. Nan gives them a thumbs-up and smiles.

"It's your new bike!" Marisol says, returning the thumbs-up. "Well, your new old bike! Or your old new bike!" She can't stop talking in exclamation points. "It used to belong to Oz, but he doesn't need it anymore so he said you could have it!" She spreads her arms wide again. "Ta-da!"

Felix's mouth makes a little O as he looks at the bike again.

It's a good bike. There are racing stripes on the

side. The seat isn't cracked or faded or anything. Besides a few little scrapes and scratches, it looks good as new.

"Wow!" says Felix. His face lights up bright, bright. He takes the handlebars from Marisol and gives the bike a once-over. "Really?"

"Yep!" Marisol says. For good measure, she adds, "Jada and I wanted to surprise you."

Felix smiles at Jada, and Jada smiles back.

"Thanks!" Felix says.

"You have to give it a name," Marisol says.

"What do you mean?" Felix asks, putting up the kickstand so he can tilt the new bike this way and that.

"My bike is named Bunny," Jada says. She motions down to her bicycle. Bunny has streamers. Bunny also has a basket, which she used to carry

Felix's gear over. "And Marisol's is named Ginny."

Felix nods like this is the most normal thing he's ever heard.

He studies the bike closely.

"I shall name him Flint," he says.

GOOD BOY

Later that evening, just before the sun sets, Marisol remembers the ball of yarn. She left it in Charlie's backseat. Mrs. Rainey says she can grab it, but she must come right back in.

Marisol doesn't even put on her socks or shoes, since she's just dashing outside quickly. She regrets it immediately, because the gravel from the driveway jabs the soft bottoms of her feet. That's why she needs to move quickly.

She opens Charlie's back door but doesn't see

anything. She climbs into the car and searches here and there until she finally spots the ball of yarn under the passenger seat. She reaches under and wiggles her fingers until they snag on the yarn. Then she pulls it out. She can't wait to give it to Beans. If he plays with it immediately, that means Felix is definitely telling the truth about communicating with animals.

She slips out of the backseat and closes the car door. She takes two steps toward the house and stops.

Her heart plummets to her feet.

Her throat goes dry.

Her stomach ties itself in a knot. A *really* tight knot.

Not a single muscle moves.

She can barely breathe.

Gregory is standing in the driveway right in front of her. His tail isn't wagging. It's hanging low. He's staring at Marisol.

Marisol's first instinct is to run, but she knows that's a bad idea.

She wants to call out for her mom or Oz or *anyone*, but she's too scared to speak.

She swallows. It feels like there's a big tennis ball stuck in her throat.

"Hi, Gregory," she says. Her voice sounds louder than she expected.

Gregory's ears perk up at the sound of his name.

His tail swishes from side to side. Not a lot. Just a bit.

"Gregory," she says again.

Swish, swish, swish.

His hackles aren't up. He's not growling. He doesn't look aggressive.

Marisol shifts her eyes away from Gregory

and turns her body to the side, just in case. But she can still see him there. She wishes her mom would come outside. She wishes she was closer to the front door. She wishes someone was there to help her. Someone braver and smarter.

She's just a girl with bare feet and a ball of yarn.

She remembers what her mom taught her.

She crouches down so she's at Gregory's level.

"Did you get lost, Gregory?" she says. The dog seems to respond to his name, so she figures she'll say it as many times as she can.

"Good boy, Gregory. Gregory is a good boy. Good Gregory."

It works. Gregory's tail is wagging properly now. He takes a step toward Marisol.

Marisol's heart goes *tha-thump, tha-thump,*

tha-thump. Her hand is getting the yarn ball all sweaty, but so be it. She stands up.

"Hi, Gregory," she says. For good measure, she adds: "I'm nice, so you don't have to eat me or anything."

Swish, swish, swish, swish, swish.

Gregory takes another step. And another.

Marisol curls her left hand into a fist and slowly, *slowly,* raises it near Gregory's nose so he can sniff her. It doesn't seem like he's mad or angry, but she's nervous, nonetheless.

He leans his narrow snout forward and sniff, sniff, sniffs her hand.

Marisol closes one eye, like she's watching a scary movie.

But nothing scary happens.

In fact, the opposite happens.

Gregory sticks out his big, long tongue and licks her hand. Then he licks it again and again. And his tail wags the whole time.

Marisol opens her other eye. Gregory steps even closer to her. He's nudging her hand, like he wants her to pet him. So she does. She scratches under his chin, remembering her mother's advice. Then she feels comfortable enough to move up to his ears.

Marisol's heart quiets down.

"Good boy, Gregory," says Marisol. "Good boy."

HOME

Gregory isn't sure what to think about the Raineys' backyard. He sniffs *everything*. Especially Peppina, which is what Marisol named the magnolia tree. When Oz comes outside to meet him, Gregory sniffs Oz's feet. Marisol feels sorry for him, because she knows what her brother's feet smell like.

Inside, Mrs. Rainey calls Gregory's owners, so they can come pick him up. Marisol stands a few feet away from Gregory while her brother pets him.

"I would have named you Bloodborn," Oz says.

Marisol wonders what she would have named Gregory. Then she remembers that she used to call him Daggers. But that doesn't seem like a good name for him anymore.

Mrs. Rainey joins them in the backyard. She puts her hands on Marisol's shoulders.

"He's not so bad, is he?" Mrs. Rainey says.

Marisol thinks about how Gregory licked her hand and wagged his tail. "No," she says. "He's not so bad."

"I'm proud of you," Mrs. Rainey whispers as they watch Oz throw a stick for the dog. Gregory doesn't fetch it. He watches the stick fly across the yard, then looks at Oz as if to say, *Was jetzt? "What next?"* Mrs. Rainey smiles at Marisol. "You were cautious *and* bold *and* responsible."

Marisol wonders if there's a dog breed out there who is all three of those things at once, but she doesn't wonder long because Gregory's owners arrive. When they ring the doorbell, Gregory's ears perk up.

"Wow, they got here fast!" Mrs. Rainey says.

Marisol follows her mother to the front door. Gregory's owners are standing on the porch. Their names are Eliot and Brandy. They have jumbled expressions on their faces. A mix of happy and worried.

"Gregory is in the backyard," Mrs. Rainey says.

"I'll show you!" Marisol offers quickly. After all, she's the one who found him. She leads Eliot and Brandy to the sliding doors that open to the backyard. The second they step outside, Gregory runs toward them as fast as he can. But Marisol's heart doesn't even go *tha-thump*, because she knows that Gregory isn't going to hurt anyone.

Brandy and Eliot crouch on the grass as Gregory attacks them with kisses. For a dog who's been missing for a while, Gregory doesn't look like he got into much trouble. He's not even dirty.

"I can't imagine how he got out of the yard," says Brandy.

"I thought dogs are supposed to be able to find their way back home," Oz says. He has another stick in his hand. He absently tosses it aside.

"Gregory is old," Brandy says, smiling and scratching the dog behind the ears. "He's not as sharp as he used to be."

When the couple stands up, Marisol notices that Eliot is crying.

"Happy tears," he explains.

Marisol has never seen a grown-up cry before, even if they're happy tears. It makes her happy, too.

"Gregory spends most of his time in the house, but he loves being in the backyard in the afternoons. You can visit him any time you want," Eliot says, looking at Marisol and Oz. "Since you're his rescuers and all."

Marisol wants to point out that she did all the work and Oz didn't do anything, but just when she opens her mouth, Oz says, "My sister is the one who found him." Then he adds: "What kind of name is Gregory for a dog, anyway?"

"He's named after Gregory Hines," Brandy says.

Oz doesn't say anything. Neither does Marisol. Neither does Mrs. Rainey. None of them know who Gregory Hines is, and none of them want to ask. Marisol reminds herself to find out later.

After Gregory Hines leaves with Brandy and Eliot, Oz goes to the refrigerator and drinks orange juice straight of the carton, even though he's not supposed to. He puts it away before Mrs. Rainey notices.

Marisol decides not to tell.

"We should get a dog," Oz says as he shuts the refrigerator door. "Can we, Mom?"

Mrs. Rainey answers quickly. "No." She looks at Marisol and winks. "Besides, we already have a Cavalier King Charles spaniel."

Oz glances between them with his eyebrows furrowed.

"Mom says that's what kind of dog I am," Marisol explains proudly. "Sweet, gentle, and affectionate."

Oz looks at Mrs. Rainey. "What kind of dog am I, Mom?"

Mrs. Rainey is already on her phone. "You are a border collie," she announces. "Agile, athletic, and active."

"Cool," Oz says.

Marisol wonders if there's a dog breed who stinks as bad as Oz after a soccer game.

She doesn't ask.

Gregory Hines, actor

one of the Best tap dancers of all time

=tap= =tap=

GINNY, BUNNY, AND FLINT

The following weekend, Marisol and Jada take Ginny and Bunny to Felix's house to see if he wants to ride bikes. Marisol plans on giving him another lesson, but he doesn't need one.

"I've been practicing all week," Felix says as he finishes gearing up. They're in the Powells' driveway, almost ready to take off. "I can ride now without falling." He snaps on his helmet, gets on Flint, and smiles at Jada. "I can't ride with one hand like you yet, but I'll get there one day."

Jada shrugs. "The most important thing is that you can ride, and now we can go on adventures together."

"What adventure are we going on today?" Felix asks.

They both look at Marisol to see if she has any ideas.

"Let's go see Gregory Hines," Marisol says. She smiles wide, from ear to ear.

"That sounds great," Felix says.

"Let's race there," Marisol suggests.

"Maybe we shouldn't," says Jada. "Since Felix just learned—"

But Felix has already taken off. "Ha! Ha!" he calls over his shoulder, going down Amaryllis like he's been bike riding his whole life.

Marisol and Jada exchange a look that says,

Let's go! They pedal and pedal and pedal. First Felix is in the lead. When they get to Tulip, Jada is first. Pretty soon, Marisol zips by both of them and sticks out her tongue. By the time they reach Gregory's fence, they're red faced and out of breath and they've forgotten to keep track of who won the race.

Gregory is sitting at the fence, like always. But this time he jumps up on all fours, wags his tail, and spins in a little circle when he sees them. He knows Marisol now, so he doesn't have to keep such a vigilant watch on her.

And she knows him, too.

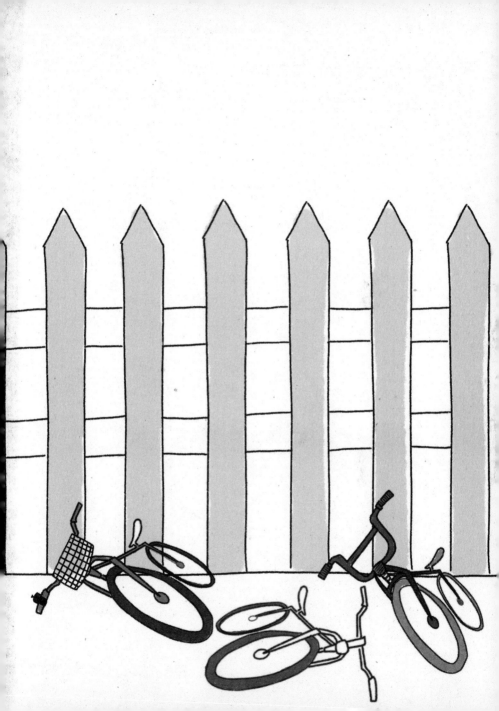

Be on the lookout for more adventures with Marisol!